JOURNEY TO CRYSTAL MOUNTAIN BOOK 2

A MIDDLE GRADE LITRPG FANTASY ADVENTURE

THE CRYSTAL MOUNTAIN SAGA
BOOK 2

TIMOTHY MCGOWEN

ILLUSTRATED BY
CANDACE MORRIS

EDITED BY
CANDACE MORRIS

RISING
TOWER
BOOKS
Fantasy / LitRPG / Gamelit

BIBLIOGRAPHY OF TIMOTHY MCGOWEN

HAVEN CHRONICLES

Haven Chronicles: Eldritch Knight

THE CRYSTAL MOUNTAIN SAGA

Journey To Crystal Mountain Book 1
Journey To Crystal Mountain Book 2

LAST BORN OF KI'DARTH

Reincarnation: A Litrpg/Gamelit Trilogy
Rebellion: A Litrpg/Gamelit Trilogy
Retribution: A Litrpg/Gamelit Trilogy

ORDER & CHAOS

Arcane Knight Book 1: An Epic LITRPG Fantasy
Arcane Knight Book 2: An Epic LITRPG Fantasy
Arcane Knight Book 3: An Epic LITRPG Fantasy
Arcane Knight Book 4: An Epic LITRPG Fantasy
Arcane Knight Book 5: An Epic LITRPG Fantasy

THE ELEMENTAL REALMS

Nexus Guardian Book 1: A Fantasy LitRPG Adventure
Nexus Guardian Book 2: A Fantasy LitRPG Adventure

REVIEWS ARE IMPORTANT

Every review matters, get your voice heard.

Follow me on Amazon to get informed when my next book is released!

https://www.amazon.com/stores/Timothy-McGowen/author/B087QTTRJK

Join my Patreon for early Chapters!

https://www.patreon.com/TimothyMcGowen

Join my Facebook group and discuss the books

https://www.facebook.com/groups/234653175151521/

SPECIAL THANKS

I wanted to give a special thanks to those that helped bring this book to its current state.

Candace Morris - Alpha Reader, Beta Reader, Editor, and Proofer

Thank you.

I dedicate this book to all my nieces and nephews, good luck on the adventures of life.

CONTENTS

BOOK 1 SUMMARY

Book 1 Summary.

Come join the crew after they are sucked into a mysterious island and set on a journey to find there way back home. Along the way they've picked up mechanical companions ready to help them figure out the way. Not to mention they've each got unique powers to help them, from Taming, Inventory, Crafting, all the way to Projecting Light out to aid their survival. But not everything is as cool as it sounds, Dinosaurs can be mighty scary and without a whole lot of teamwork you might find yourself in over your head. But Addy, Zack, Sofia, and Jayden are quickly becoming fast friends when faced against the impossible odds. Follow their journey into book 2 where they must uncover more secrets to how to escape the dangerous dinosaur filled island.

CHAPTER 1
ZACK – WE DID IT!

"I'm telling you guys, if we are going to go into a cave, we need at least a week's worth of supplies. We should be prepared," I said, not that anyone was really disagreeing with me, but it needed to be said.

Addy looked me square in the face, her dark eyes so intelligent and keen. She sighed and her jet-black hair, with streaks of pink, bounced as she did so.

She was tall for our age; she'd even passed me up and I was basically the tallest boy in our class. She carried herself with confidence befitting the daughter of a pair of doctors. She used to remind everyone that would listen that she, like her parents, would be a doctor one day. With how crazy my home life was, I'd been to her parents' clinic several times for strains and even a broken bone or two.

There used to be a time that I considered us fast friends, but times had changed. Of course, with our newest adventure into the unknown, I'd grown much closer to her, but there was still a distance that I couldn't put my finger on. It was like we both saw ourselves as the leader of our little band of misfits, but neither would admit defeat to the other. As much as I didn't want to admit it, she was probably better suited for the job, but darn it, I wanted to be the one to give orders. It just felt right to me. Plus, that would mean no one could tell me what to do, and that always meant a good time.

She'd said something and my loud inner thoughts had made me miss it. I inclined my head to the side and looked at her until she realized that I hadn't heard her. With a big huff of air and a stomped foot she repeated herself.

"What are we going to do about that T-Rex or something worse if it returns while we are on the ground? I'm worried about going into a cave and not having a way out," Addy said, she always thought of the best questions, but I had an answer for her this time.

Ash, my pet mechanical bird, nudged my face and I felt through our bond that he wanted me to voice my thoughts concerning the T-Rex and the red eyes. Whatever or wherever these little mechanized friends came from, I felt like they had our best interest at heart, and they wanted us to escape this place as badly as we did. I took Ash, he was so much like the bird my father used to have and cleared my throat.

"I don't think the T-Rex will be an issue anymore," I announced as if saying as much would be enough to calm everyone. It, of course, wasn't and Jayden was the first to voice his objection.

"Uhm, excuse my words of dissent, but what facts do you have to support your hypothesis that the T-Rex isn't a threat any longer?" Jayden asked in the most Jayden way possible. Of course, he looked much more threatening with his raptor Charles at his side, he was a tamer and had added the scary looking dino to our team earlier that day. He'd even been able to heal it up fast with a few extra rations of food. Unfortunately, his dodos hadn't made it through the fight, instead becoming food for the T-Rex.

"In English please," Sofia said, her sour look shining through. She always had that rich girl sour look on her face. It was like she thought she was too good to help or something. Recently she'd begun helping and learned that she had the coolest and lamest power of us all, Inventory. During the fight she'd dropped large loads of stuff on the T-Rex's head, which proved to be more useful that any of us had imagined.

Jayden was super interested in it, but I'd been less enthusiastic about it. Like, it *was* a lifesaver, and we couldn't have done so much of our recent building projects without it but come on. Jayden had said something about the limitless potential of storage, but I didn't really follow his train of thought. Even Addy had looked a bit lost when he went into how such a device must operate.

"Jayden wants to know why you think the T-Rex isn't

a threat," Addy offered, folding her arms in front of herself. "You saw the eye too, huh?"

I put the hood up on my red sweater and rolled my eyes. Everyone wanted to question me, and no one could just accept that I was right, just like at home. Sighing, I decided to explain what I'd seen. I went over how at the end of the attack, when it looked like we were going to beat the T-Rex and finally be rid of it, its undamaged eye had gone from a glowing red to a normal look. It had even looked confused, I told them, maybe even a bit scared as the raptors chased it away.

"So, you see," I said, finishing with my long explanation, "he or I guess it could be a she, but anyways the Rex isn't a threat unless it gets those glowing red eyes. I think something was controlling it, maybe Mr. Shadow?"

I could see that I'd convinced Jayden and Addy, but Sofia remained suspicious.

"I saw the eyes too," Jayden said, nodding his head as he adjusted his thick-rimmed glasses. He wore an Einstein with his tongue out t-shirt and khaki shorts with obvious scrapes on his legs from our adventures. We each had our backpacks as well, but with Sofia's Inventory skill they were probably not needed. Jayden's amber-colored eyes regarded me before he finished his thought. "I didn't see the red go away, but it would stand to reason that if they did go away and then it ran, there could be potential mind control going on. Maybe something similar to how I can tame dinosaurs now? It stands to reason that we should at the very least consider Zack's words."

He took a lot of words to simply say that I was right, and they should listen to me, but I didn't bug him about it. Jayden was one of my closest friends, if not for him I don't even know if I'd be able to pass most of my classes.

"I saw it too, Zack," Addy said, raising her hands up in front of her as she spoke. "We need to keep our eyes open for anything with red eyes. That seems simple enough. But what if we find ourselves cornered inside the cave by red eyes? Maybe we ought to wait it out on the beach for a few days and someone will come to rescue us." She held a hand on her robotic monkey, Cappy, then sighed. "Cappy doesn't think that is likely to help. I guess I'm in for going to the cave, but we should be prepared like Zack suggested."

With most of the group in agreement I began to give out commands before Addy could do the same. I told Jayden to come with me to gather more meat and water. I sent Addy and Sofia to gather wood, stone, and other basic items like roots and leaves, that I could use to make all manner of items once I figured out how with my crafting magic. Thinking about crafting caused an itch on my arm where the magical bracelet thingy was attached to my right wrist. I strained my brain to remember what it had been called but settled for just checking it by touching it.

. . .

Creation Matrix: Level 5, 15% Experience toward the next Level, 30/30 Charges Remaining.

Equipped Item: Band of Elkor (Soul Band) A device created by an Ancient Warrior to aid him in the creation of matter from a variety of supplies. It can channel matter together to create new items.

Well, that was new, I thought as I ran my hand over it. I hadn't seen this new display that gave it a specific name before, so that was cool. Band of Elkor had a cool ring to it, almost familiar like from a book I might have listened to at some point. My father used to listen to a lot of books during long car drives back when he was still around, maybe from one of those. I zoned out while going to work, killing more of the birds so that we could cook them and store them away. Jayden called them dodo birds, but I just thought of them as lunch.

CHAPTER 2
ADDY – GATHER SUPPLIES

Z ack was trying to take charge again, but I was too tired from the day's ordeal to fight him over it. He even had a few good points so it made sense to let him have a few wins, it would help his confidence. Sofia itched at her left arm where her Soul Band was located, and I wondered if it grew heavier the more we collected items or if it felt normal. I made a note in my head to ask her about it later when we were alone. As per her usual she was collecting the least amount of supplies but was more than willing to wait and take items from me. She acted as if putting items away were a chore enough.

She had dark auburn hair and beautiful olive-colored skin. Her slight accent always got the boys' attention, it was very exotic despite just being a normal Italian accent. Her curls were in disarray, but I couldn't tell her as she was about ready to sit down and give up already. She cared so much about what she looked like, not that I didn't, but nowhere near how much Sofia did. She caught my eyes and smiled, but it didn't reach her eyes. It was the smile she put on when she was frustrated and wanted nothing more than to go relax.

Sofia and I had been close friends for a while now and I felt like I knew her best of all. However, she was not the person I'd have chosen to go on a magical adventure with, in fact none of my current company would be in my first picks. Sure, Zack could be useful, and he was pretty strong, resourceful when he wanted to be, but his need to be in charge rubbed me the wrong way.

Jayden, in theory, was a good choice. Knowledgeable, keen minded, and a solid team player, but he was so scared all the time that it hardly mattered. However, he'd gotten a firm hold on his fear after adding a real freaking raptor to his side, Charles he named it. I guess a large attack dinosaur would be enough to make anyone a little confident. I watched Sofia's snake and wondered if she'd even decided to name it. Reaching out to touch its robotic skin, it turned and hissed at me.

Sofia turned and looked at my outstretched hand with a raised brow. "Sorry, he's protective. Aren't you my little snaky poo," she rubbed her nose against the snake's, and I scrunched my own nose in disgust. I wasn't a fan of snakes, truth be told, but Sofia seemed happy enough with it.

I looked over to my little monkey man, Cappy, and

felt his comforting thoughts press against my own. There was something going on with these little robot animal companions, I wasn't a fool, but it was hard to care when all they seemed to want from us was to comfort and protect. You try pushing away something that made you feel safe and calm, it wasn't easy. Not to mention we were all alone and facing threats like real life dinosaurs. No. I'd rather have Cappy at my side than not.

After spending several long minutes filling Sofia with all the supplies that we could, we left to go back to the base we'd built on the beach. It was a wonderful little tree-house base, and I almost couldn't believe we'd been able to build it. Of course, without the help from Zack and Sofia we wouldn't have been able to do it at all. The T-Rex had done some damage to it, but it had been easy enough to fix after it ran off. They had interesting powers provided to them, but somehow, I'd ended up with the only really offensive and defensive tool, hard light.

I thought I remembered seeing, just in passing of course, a cartoon that dealt with hard light. Something about using a ring and emotions to control it. That didn't really apply here, but I had created a new skill on the fly when I attacked the T-Rex and I hadn't checked my display yet to see what it had said about it.

Light Weaver: Level 5, 19% Experience toward the next Level, 30/30 Charges.

New Skill Unlocked! Light Javelin: Create a solid Light construct in the shape of a Javelin. It takes 2 Charges to Create.

I'd leveled from my fight against the T-Rex! That was good news, and I couldn't help but pump my fist into the air in triumph. I could almost hear my mother's words in my head telling me not to celebrate too soon and then my father quipping back that I ought to celebrate all victories no matter how small. Neither were wrong of course; it would be wise to be both prudent and quick to celebrate when in a situation that seemed so impossible. I can't imagine that either of my parents had ever been through an ordeal like this, so instead of worrying so much, I ought to be grateful to have a chance to learn in such a unique way.

I pushed a large prehistoric looking leaf out of the way and couldn't help but wonder what lesson I ought to learn from this experience. Don't upset mysterious substitute teachers who had the power to send you to a dangerous island filled with dinosaurs? Or perhaps, with the power of friendship we can overcome anything! Neither seemed like legit reasons and I couldn't help but shake my head at the ridiculousness of our situation.

"Do you have enough charges to put this into your inventory?" Zack asked Sofia, she just shrugged and took large piles of cooked meat from him. With how the Soul

Bands leveled, I was sure her using her inventory so much likely had gotten her to level 5 as well, if not higher. I didn't want to bug her into checking, as she preferred to ignore her 'unsightly' bracelet as she called it.

"All out of charges for a few hours," Sofia announced as the last of the waterskins disappeared into her arm. "So, about this trip to the cave..." She bit her lip and looked about nervously.

"What is it?" I asked, putting a friendly hand on her arm, but staying away from the snake to be safe.

"How dark do you think it'll be?" She asked, her voice quavering ever so slightly.

Oh shoot, I'd totally forgotten about this. Not only was she not a fan of heights, but she also 'preferred' not to be in total darkness if at all possible.

I smiled and summoned forth a globe of light. "Don't worry, I can keep these up indefinitely," I said, beaming with my best smile. I really wanted to make sure she didn't freak out when we got to the cave, but it would be hard to say if we wouldn't have to go into darkness at some point, for our own safety. Unfortunately, Zack had the sense of a blind bat and didn't understand Sofia's fear.

"What, are you afraid of the dark or something?" he asked, immediately laughing and elbow Jayden who had enough sense to look at his feet.

Sofia turned on him, her face going red. "You listen here you little worm! If you think I am afraid of anything, you can just throw yourself off a cliff. I'm just concerned that we might... uhh... get lost in a dark cave. It isn't smart to get lost inside a cave when rescue might come here to the beach. I vote we stay here, who's with me?"

I bit my lip, not wanting to give Zack anything else to work with, nor wanting to betray the trust Sofia had put in me, but before I could say anything he ran his mouth again, digging himself deeper into a hole everyone could see but him.

"Don't be a scaredy cat, the darkness won't get you. Maybe a dinosaur in the dark or something, but not the dark. Gosh, I can't believe you are afraid of the dark, what a girl. Can you believe this Jayden?" Zack said, full of the stupid confidence that he held like a shield in front of himself.

"I think a fear of the dark in this situation is completely reasonable and you making fun of her is extremely rude," Jayden said, taking a step away from his friend.

Zack looked absolutely shocked at his friend's betrayal and opened and closed his mouth several times. Before he could say anything more I cut in.

"Together we can make it through anything, we've learned that lesson already, right? The map showed us the way because we agreed it was the right thing to do. We need to be supportive of each other and not make fun of our fears," I said the last bit while staring hard at Zack, hoping my point would come across. It didn't, and Zack just looked angry at all of us now.

I saw the beginning of tears welling up in Zack's eyes before he turned and made his way out of the treehouse and into the forest. "I'm going to the cave, with or without you guys." He called up to us and we all sighed, reluctantly following him. The sun was still high in the sky, and I dismissed my ball of light as it wasn't really lighting anything. Even so, I saw Sofia twitch as I did so. This was going to be a hard adventure and I wasn't sure I could keep us from falling apart.

CHAPTER 3
ZACK – ARMING UP

What did they know about fears. I felt red hot shame on my face as tears threatened to cascade down my cheeks. It seemed like no matter how hard I tried or where I went, I was always the troublemaker. I hadn't meant to tease Sofia about being afraid of the dark, sometimes I just can't help myself. Now how would I be the leader if they thought of me as a bully? Everything was ruined and now I was walking through the woods alone.

A gentle nuzzle on my neck caught my attention and I felt a warm buzz travel throughout my body. Things weren't so bad after all, I realized. I had my buddy Ash, and he would keep me safe. I heard noises behind me, and I let out a breath of air. They were following me toward the cave after all. Jayden hurried to catch up to me and I slowed to let him.

"You okay?" Jayden asked, adjusting his thick glasses.

That question nearly pulled me over the edge to tears, but I held on to my emotions, forcing them down. I had to stay strong for the group, they needed a strong leader. Turning to Jayden I answered him.

"Yeah, why wouldn't I be," I said, trying not to sound so angry and failing.

"Just checking in on you," Jayden said, putting a friendly hand on my shoulder. "Can I give you a word of advice?"

I looked over at him. Jayden was a good friend and I teased him more than anyone else some days, but he always stuck by my side. If I could trust anyone to give decent advice, it would be my best friend Jayden. But something inside of me rebelled against the idea of advice or someone telling me what to do. I didn't know what it was or why I acted the way I did sometimes, but I did my best to push the thoughts down and trust my friend. I found that I actually wanted to hear what he had to say, the sudden change in my mood surprised me.

"I guess," I said, not wanting to sound too overly eager to hear what he had to say.

"If you want to be a leader, then try to emulate other good leaders."

"Emulate?" I asked, looking at him like he'd started speaking Latin or something.

"Do what they do," Jayden quickly amended then continued. "For example, a good leader will listen to others and be careful not to make fun of their fears. In fact, I think good leaders' comfort or reinforce someone who has fears. I'm afraid of a lot and it doesn't help to have it laughed at."

"I didn't laugh at you," I said, feeling attacked by his line of comments. That familiar anger at being challenged rising again in my chest.

"No, but you did make Sofia feel like she was wrong for being afraid of the dark. If we are going to make it through this in one piece, we have to be a cohesive unit," Jayden said, once more adding words that I barely understood. I understood cohesive by the context, but man Jayden must have a word of the day calendar back home or something, he knew so many words I didn't. But like I said, the context helped, and I wasn't going to ask him to explain, otherwise he might think I was dumb. And I was no dummy.

"I get it," I admitted, then shrugged. "I guess I can tell her I'm sorry."

"A good leader might do just that," Jayden said, smiling wide.

Turning, I saw Sofia and Addy walking together only ten feet or so behind us, far enough away that they hadn't picked up on our conversation. Addy glared in my direction when she saw me looking and Sofia still had her eyes towards the ground.

Reluctantly, I slowed my pace enough for them to catch up to me. The last thing I wanted to do was admit I was wrong, but Jayden was right. If I wanted to be a good leader I needed to step up and follow the example of a good leader.

"Hey Sofia, could I, uh, talk to you alone for a second?" I asked, biting my lower lip, and waiting for the inevitable rejection. Sofia was a pretty girl and even out here in the jungle island we'd got ourselves caught in, I felt my face grow hot just like when I tried to talk to girls back at school.

She looked up, her beautiful eyes reflecting tears that had gathered there and her almost always perfect hair bouncing as she shook her head no. I'd expected as much, but Addy surprised me by speaking up.

"I'm going to go see what Jayden is up to, I'll be right back, okay Sofia?" Then as quickly as she'd spoken, she jogged away leaving us alone.

I took up step beside her and couldn't look her in the face. She'd been so mean to me so many times. So what if I'd called her out about her fears? But what was she feeling being in this situation? It wasn't often I spent time considering other people's feelings, but in this case, I thought it was what a leader would do, so I tried my best to imagine what all this meant to her.

She was used to being pampered and I knew for a fact her parents were rich. I bet she hadn't even gone camping, not real camping out in the dirt and muck of it all. To be so suddenly thrown into a situation where you had to rely on others for your safety—and then there were her powers. Of all the powers she could be given, she got inventory. She'd probably gone from feeling useless to feeling like all she could contribute was to carry things. Then when she tried to ask about something she was afraid of, I made fun of her.

Man, I could really be a jerk sometimes and I didn't like that about myself. So, I was going to step up and do what a leader should do, make it right.

"Sofia," I said, gathering my thoughts to figure out the best way to say this. "I'm sorry that I made fun of your fear of the dark. It was mean of me to do that, and I don't think it helps our group for me to be like that. I mean, you are probably right to be afraid of the dark anyways, all sorts of things could be down there, and we don't exactly have the best track record of keeping wild things away. I guess what I'm trying to say, is that I'm sorry and I'll try to be more sensitive in the future."

I spared a glance at her and saw that she was full on crying now, tears silently running down her cheeks. She stopped and so I did. Looking at me, she smiled and then she surprised me. She hugged me, burying her face into my shoulder and began to sob. I looked all around for help, seeing Addy and Jayden had stopped and were looking at us now, but they were no help.

Addy noticed and she put an odd sort of smile on her face like she was watching a puppy play or something. Jayden readjusted his thick glasses and gave me a thumbs up. The awkward hug and cry session only lasted a few more seconds, but I felt good about it.

"Thank you," she said, then ran to join Addy and Jayden up ahead, leaving me alone with my thoughts.

I'd never felt that kind of warmth before, not like that at least, and I think I liked it. Being nice and trying to do the right thing might just be my thing after all. Instead of trying to think about the next funny joke or silly thing I could do, I tried to think about what I could do next as our leader to make me feel like that inside again. But I was new to this and came up short, eventually jogging to join my teammates in this twisted game of fate.

I pulled out the map and gave it a solid look before rolling it back up again. We were only a mile or so from the cave so we should reach it with plenty of light still in the sky. My mind wandered when I considered the cave and what might be waiting for us inside. I had the power to make some basic stone tools, so I figured maybe we should take a break so I could make everyone a stone machete or something.

"Hey, let's take a break so I can make some weapons for all of us. The stone machete would be useful for all of us if we got into a fight," I said, feeling good about my quick thinking. Unfortunately, Addy immediately cut me off.

"You nearly took your arm off; I don't like the idea of each of us having a weapon. Plus, my light abilities are offense enough for me. Maybe if you could make a club or something?" Addy asked and I scratched my chin, thinking about it. I didn't like that Addy was trying to take charge or decide how I should do things, but she was right, a club might be the more effective weapon after all.

I had leveled up to 5 from the traps and stuff I'd been doing but I hadn't really tried to learn any more new recipes. So, this ought to be a good time to try. When I placed my hand on the Soul Band the usual information appeared, but I went to the crafting menu, focusing on what I wanted.

New Crafting Branch Unlocked! Basic Arms and Armor: Through the power of your Soul Band (Creation Matrix) you can now make basic Arms and Armor up to copper rank.

"Heck yes!" I said, pumping a fist into the air. Quickly, I scrolled through to see what I could make and what I couldn't. With hides, like the kind I'd gotten from the dodo's, I could make basic leather armor; a set included a cap, chest piece, pants and belt, gloves, and boots. Then there were the weapons! I could make a stone sword, stone club, stone spear, and a stone axe that had two sides and wasn't meant for cutting wood. I could also see that if I got some copper I'd be able to make better weapons, so I decided to make a pickaxe just in case we came across some copper in the cave.

I only had enough hides to make a couple pieces of

armor, but I had plenty of supplies to make any of the weapons. Sharing with the group, it was decided that we would wait until an entire suit could be made before we did the armor, and instead, focus on making weapons meant for defense.

Addy decided that she'd take a spear, just in case her Soul Band ran out of charges mid fight. Jayden went with a club, saying he didn't like the idea of getting cut when he tried to attack things. His raptor, Charles, looked at the club appraisingly and I swear it approved of the weapon. Meanwhile, Sofia surprised me by asking for a sword.

"I've got years of experience fencing," she said, smiling and finally seeming to get over the watery eyes that had been plaguing her.

I also wanted a sword and so I crafted two of them. They were simple things, the wood made up the handle and black razor-sharp stone had been embedded into the side of the wooden shaft all the way up to make a 'sort of sword'.

"That looks like a macuahuitl," Jayden said, his eyes wide.

I had no idea what or how to even say the word he just said, so I just nodded. It was basically a wooden bat with sharp stone added to the edges, not at all the sword I was imagining.

"This is a bit different from my fencing sword, but I'll make do," Sofia said, her mood much lighter than it had been since we arrived. Maybe my apology had really done some good after all. "But don't expect me to teach you how to use it." She added, a bit of her old snark back in her voice.

I had just been about to ask her to do just that, so my mood soured, and I increased my pace to take the lead back from Addy and her spear.

CHAPTER 4
ADDY – FINDING A PLACE TO REST

Z ack hustled past me, making sure he was in the lead, typical Zack behavior. I rolled my eyes but decided to say nothing, as he had shown some backbone in talking to Sofia. The spear he'd given me worked well as a walking stick, but I couldn't help but eye the tip with a sense of danger. Despite how I felt older than I was at times, I was still barely a preteen and we really shouldn't have weapons. But this was the life we'd been thrown into, dangerous dinosaurs, magic, and adventure.

We finally made it to the cave. It was the same as I remembered from before, a large opening and a clearing separated by trees with a small waterfall filling a bowl shape in the rock with pure water. Zack, despite his need to create weapons, had also made several waterskins, which we filled with the pure water before venturing deeper into the cave. Remnants of when we stayed here before could still be seen, but no T-Rex, so that was good at least. I didn't know what we'd do without Jayden and the help his raptor had provided.

"I'm taking lead here," I said, summoning forth a globe of light. "Stay within the circle of light and be ready for anything."

My instructions were crystal clear, but of course I saw Zack roll his eyes and step up right next to me, not willing to be a step behind when he saw himself as the leader. One of his biggest flaws that I was beginning to see with him was his unwillingness to let others take command. Like we wanted the class clown to be in charge anyways. Not even Jayden, his closest friend, would want that. But it was what it was, and I was stuck in competition with him.

I held up the light in my right hand and held the spear like a walking stick in my left. Just as we'd thought, the cave opened up after narrowing to the point where Zack was forced to let me go first or risk cutting me with his cricket bat with rocks set into the side. Jayden knew what it was called, but that wasn't surprising because Jayden seemed to know everything. Sure, I was a little jealous, but Cappy put a gentle hand on my head and it didn't seem so bad.

Cappy was a great little companion and I wondered what would happen if we escaped this place. Would the magic and Cappy stay behind? Suddenly I didn't know how invested I was in leaving and it scared me a little. Like I felt a closeness with Cappy that I hadn't ever felt before and I wanted him to come with me to the world of science and logic, despite that not being logical at all. Suddenly I felt like I was one of the characters on my father's favorite show, Star Trek. The pointy eared guy who always talked about logic and reasoning.

To be fair, I actually liked the few episodes I'd seen, but we had so little time to do much actual TV watching that I never got a chance to learn much about it. Which just went even further to remind me that I ought to be at home studying, but instead I was wandering through a moist cave after getting detention for the first time ever. What are the chances the universe cared about my chances of becoming a doctor at all? Seriously, all I'd done was laugh at a stupid joke, by a silly boy.

I shot Zack a glare but in the dim light cast from my globe I wasn't even sure if he saw it. "When we get out of here," I said, keeping my voice a low whisper. "If that Mr. Shadow guy is still around, then you need to apologize to him before he sends us someplace else. Got it?" I tried not to be bossy but everything Zack did made me want to give him a better way or some instructions. Boys were just the worst.

I smiled at that thought. Sofia and I used to think the same, but recently she'd begun to enjoy the company of boys, much to my dismay. Like what was so special about noisy, dirty, smelly, boys? Yuck. But then I thought of the times Zack had stepped up and really came through for us against the T-Rex, but no, no, no,

I'd been the one throwing spears of light and whatnot. If anything, he should have thanked me for all I did to help, but did he?

No. He. Did. Not.

My frustration grew with each thought until I finally had to just let out a sigh. I was just thinking myself in circles and that was going to do me no good. Cappy agreed, I could feel his impressions in my head and once more I hoped beyond hope that he'd find his way back with us. Might be hard to explain to my parents, but I'd be willing to try.

The darkness ahead opened up as the tunnel widened into a vast cavern filled with stalagmites and stalactites. My globe of light only filled an area of about twenty feet around us, then the light faded to almost nothing, but as far as I could see it was just an open cave system. Then I saw the red dots begin to appear in the distance.

"Be very quiet," I said, a tremble in my voice as I gestured with my spear at the dozen or so red lights in the distance.

"Those are pretty small, perhaps just bats?" Jayden said, squinting toward the darkness but keeping his voice low.

Even Zack had the presence of mind to keep his voice low as he rejoined my side and looked off into the distance. "Weapons ready and spread out some more." He immediately began giving orders like he was some kind of general or something. I rolled my eyes, but followed his lead because I didn't want to get hit by his weapon if he started swinging it around.

"Uhm, can you make more of those lights?" Sofia asked, her breathing was heavy and despite trying to whisper she'd been twice as loud as any of us. Another dozen or so red eyes joined the group ahead.

That wasn't a bad idea. I rolled my light away from me and she picked it up as it rolled right up to her foot. Focusing I created another one and this one I rolled over to Jayden, then Zack, and finally I made one for myself, but I set it on the ground a few feet away. I didn't know much about using a spear, but if I was going to use it then I'd use two hands.

I counted a dozen pairs of eyes and suddenly the beating of wings. They were coming and we had to be ready. But the first wave of, well whatever they were, passed right overhead and toward the exit behind us. I let out a deep breath, thinking that we were out of the woods, so to speak, but then the cave around us began to rumble.

It was like the very ground all around us didn't like that we were inside the cave, and it shook to force us to flee. I picked up my light and bit my lower lip, what should we do?

"Let's go deeper, the stone has to be down here some-where," Zack said and this time I was too afraid to do anything but listen to him.

We began walking deeper but stayed to the edge of the cave wall. The darkness combined with the utter silence put my nerves on edge, but I kept one foot in front of the other. At some point, Sofia and I took each other's hands, her free hand holding a light and her sword nowhere to be seen.

"Can you read this?" Jayden asked, making me jump from the sudden break in the silence. I turned to see what he was referring to and my head tilted to the side upon seeing the text.

The wall was covered in caveman-style finger drawings with images of what must have been bats, and something that looked like a spider, as well as a long tube that might represent the tunnel, but the words written beneath it was unlike anything I'd studied. Perhaps a type of ideographic system like Chinese or Japanese, but I knew a little of both and there was just a strangeness to the symbols that baffled my brain. The longer I stared at them, the less I felt I could understand them. This was beyond frustrating for me. I'd made it a point to be well versed in the basics of so many languages, why wasn't this in Latin like the map and the message that sent us to this cave?

Then, as if in answer to my pleas, I saw a bit of Latin that I recognized.

"Est periculum hic," I said, working over what it meant in my head. "Roughly means, danger here or there's danger here."

"Tell me something I don't know," Zack said, chuckling and nudging his elbow playfully into Jayden who just flinched as if struck.

"The eyes are back," Sofia said, sounding like she was going to scream at any moment. She let my hand go and a weapon appeared in her left hand.

"Spread out and swing as hard as you can," Zack commanded, and we all listened.

CHAPTER 5
ZACK – FIRST OBSTACLE

The red eyes were back, and they descended on us like a wall of twinkling lights. Addy had stated the obvious and it was like a call to the red eyes that we wanted to fight, or at least that's how I saw it. The bats, because I could finally see what they were, came right for us and we got ready.

It was just like the situation with the dodos, I had to get my hands dirty. Many of the red-eyed bats, the size of small breed dogs, flew right over our heads and away, but a couple circled, and I couldn't help but think they were looking for our weakest link. Jayden's club shook from fear and the two pairs of eyes locked onto him, diving low.

"Jayden! Watch out!" I shouted, rushing forward with my sword. He dropped his club and hit the ground, but Charles—his raptor—had other plans. It jumped much higher than I would have thought possible and grabbed hold of one of the bats. I caught the other with the flat of my paddle-like sword. It hit the ground with a solid thump, but suddenly the air was filled with a screeching sound. I turned to see that dozens of pairs of eyes had turned and were coming right for us.

"Time to run!" I shouted, there was no way we could fight that many at once. Reaching down, I helped Jayden up and the four of us began to run deeper into the cave. A smaller opening appeared before us; the light and shadows were almost enough to make us miss it, but Sofia called out and we huddled into it.

The bats flew by, unwilling or unable to get to us into our new little hideout. Charles breathed heavily on the back of my neck, and I couldn't help but wonder when Jayden had last fed the creature. Hopefully the bat meal would be enough to hold his raptor together. We'd be toast if that raptor turned on us—suddenly I felt the need for Charles to have another meal.

"Sofia, give Jayden meat to feed his raptor," I said, my voice shaky despite doing my best to make it sound strong. Charles looked down at me as I spoke, and I swear it looked hungry.

"Don't bother," Jayden said, his voice still a whisper and his heavy breathing making it hard to understand him.

"He might have a point," Addy said, supporting me for once, a surprise for sure.

"I can feel our bond," Jayden insisted. "He's good, that bat counted as a meal I provided."

"What are we going to do about the blood sucking bats?" I asked, my brain struggling to figure out a plan and coming up empty. This was next level trouble; they could so easily outnumber us and we had no way to heal or bandage like they did in games... oh man we were in trouble.

"We don't know that they are blood sucking," Addy assured me, hands in front of her as if trying to calm me down.

"We don't know that they aren't," I insisted, lifting my sword, and peeking out of our little hidey-hole. Then a thought occurred to me. "Jayden, do you think you could tame one and then maybe they'll leave us alone?"

"We'd have to get one to eat from me and I don't know whether Charles will let one close without eating it first. He really enjoyed the taste," Jayden said, shifting uncomfortably under my gaze.

"Then what are our options?" I asked, again unable to come up with anything myself. For once I found myself wanting and needing to hear from the others what the best way forward might be. I rarely relied on others if I could help it, but this was a situation where the voices of others were welcomed.

"We run for it," Addy said, her eyes running over each of us in turn.

It was a fair plan, but it hurt to think of us running

from a challenge. There had to be a way to solve this little issue without just taking off. Of course, running had served us greatly in the past so why change up the routine that worked? As I watched more bats swooped down, getting closer to our hideout than before, I decided that it might be the only choice.

There was a way out of this, but it wasn't easy for me to accept that it meant running. I cleared my throat and tightened my grip around my sword. There was going to be a fight even if we ran, so we might as well be ready for it. Between my sword and Jayden's raptor, we had a chance of getting out. Of course, I'd need to show myself to be awesome with a weapon that I knew very little about, but I could manage.

With a plan formed in my head I turned to Addy and the others. "We will make a run for it. If we get to the outside of the cave, we can have Jayden tame more dinos and come back in force. Jayden, you keep your raptor toward the back with me so we can take out any attacking bats while we run. Got it?"

Everyone nodded, some slower than others. Addy obviously didn't like me taking charge, but she hadn't offered up a better plan, so we would stick with what we had. So, making myself ready, I squashed down my worry and signaled for the team to run.

With what little light we had, Addy took off first, leading the way. I trailed with Charles the raptor at my side, occasionally looking behind us for signs of attackers.

We'd made it a fair distance when the screeching started. It sent shivers down my spine, and I hate to admit that I began to feel afraid. Ash rubbed against my neck and suddenly a wave of warmth went through me. My task didn't seem so impossible anymore. In fact, I felt so brave I actually turned and stopped, ready to take on the bats by myself.

Charles took my cue and turned to fight as well. That was when the ground began to rumble, and the bugs appeared. First to appear was a centipede, long and gross with so many legs. It dug right out of the ground, followed by a blue beetle, and an oversized ant. Each insect was the size of a cat at least and suddenly my newfound courage faltered.

But I wasn't going to fail so easily! I rushed forward and smashed my sword into the biggest of the bugs, the centipede. Its body squelched in with a satisfactory smash and I was moving to the next target. I disposed of three insects before the bats reached us and the ground began to rumble again.

Swinging high, I missed one but beamed another bat in the face, tearing it from the sky.

"It's working!" I cried out to no one in particular. Charles grabbed one out of the air as well, but not before taking a few cuts and screeching out a little sound of his own. I hoped he wasn't calling for backup again, because I wasn't safely up in a tree this time.

The swarm came back around just as a few more

insects arrived. Diving to the side, I missed getting hit by a giant grasshopper, but I got scratched by one of the swooping bats. I grimaced in pain, but it wasn't so bad. Kind of like when I scraped my knee, which I did all too often. Clumsily I searched for my fallen weapon and my hand fell around it just in time to strike down a swooping bat. *This is amazing!* I thought as I did my best to keep the enemy at bay.

Just when things were getting a good rhythm, several more insects arrived and suddenly Charles and I weren't going to be enough. Traps, I could make traps, or craft something that might be useful! But no, there was no time for that now and the traps I'd made were with Sofia. How was I going to get out of this mess I'd gotten myself in?

Just as one of the insects attacked, getting through my own attack, I closed one eye, preparing myself for the pain. The pain didn't come, instead, a flash of light filled the area with new illumination, and I was saved.

"Thought you could use a hand," Addy said, swirling a javelin of light that seemed to spark with dangerous potential.

"Attack bugs, go!" Jayden yelled and three ants appeared from behind him, joining the fight. He winked at me when I looked back at him and I felt like I was meeting Jayden for the first time, so confident and ready to do battle.

Sofia stood in the back with her sword held

awkwardly, and her expression fearful. It was enough that most of us had joined the battle though, and the tide quickly began to shift. One by one we took out the bats and the bugs, and with each swing we made progress.

CHAPTER 6
ADDY – OVERCOMING FEARS

I slashed out with my spear of light and hit a bug right in the face, ending it. There was so much going on but by this point I let the thrill of battle take over and I barely noticed as the fight changed in our favor. Slashing and poking, I watched as the three ants Jayden had swiftly tamed—he used a new type of taming that just suddenly appeared for him when he was concentrating. He'd said it was temporary for now, but he had at least a dozen minutes or so of control over the ants. Something about them being insects made it possible to tame without traditional feeding methods but not for as long.

We'd had to turn around when the tunnel ahead was blocked by rock and debris, then the bugs came. Luckily, we'd turned around just in time to see Zack nearly overtaken by a swarm of cave creatures. Now we were finally in the fight of our lives, and we were winning.

I slashed low at an ant, taking its leg off before swirling the spear around and smashing in its head. It wasn't the cleanest bit of work, but somehow, I found myself enjoying it. Even Sofia came up to strike down a centipede that tried to come at me from the side while I was looking the other way.

"Thank you," I said, smiling at her as she stepped back to the relative safety of the backlines.

The cave was dark, save for the light orbs I'd created for us, they'd been discarded on the ground rolling here and there as we fought. If it weren't for the close quarters of the tunnel Zack had decided to fight in, we'd have likely been overwhelmed by now. But that wasn't what was happening. No. Instead we were actually making some headway in the fight and slowly and but surely, we were winning.

"Watch out!" Zack called, slashing at a bat that dove for me, but missing it.

I was ready, throwing my javelin of light and following it up by shooting out a beam of light at a beetle sneaking up on Jayden. He gave me a grateful smile, which I returned before focusing back on the battle. Just a little bit longer and we'll have won the fight against the red-eyed bats and bugs.

What had made the bugs here so large? I found myself wondering as I fought. It was easy now, the last of the bats had fled and the largest of the bugs were down. It was all about moving forward as a unit and stomping out the cat-sized beetles that were left. One such beetle, an iridescent red, appeared in the back line and began to glow.

"Something is happening!" Zack called out, swinging fast as he tried to reach the glowing beetle before it could do whatever it was trying to do.

"Captain obvious," Sofia said, coming to stand beside me as I readied a spear for the glowing beetle. At the last moment, I changed my mind.

"Get back, quick!" I called out, raising a shield in front of Zack a moment before it happened.

The glowing beetle let out a screech and fire, bright and furious, streamed out from its mouth, covering the spot where Zack had been moments before. I could feel the strain to maintain the barrier, but I kept it up and crossed my fingers that Zack would be alright.

"Oh no," Jayden said as the fire cut out and our eyes struggled to adjust to lower light from my orbs. What had happened? Was Zack okay?

The smoke cleared and Charles the raptor rushed forward, ending the final beetle before it could let off any more fire. My barrier shattered from a sudden force, and I heard Zack coughing. Rushing forward, I found him on a knee, his sword held out as if he was still ready for battle.

"Are you okay?" I asked, putting a hand on his shoulder.

"I'm fine," Zack said after coughing several times. "Hard to breathe inside that bubble, I had to pop it. Did you take out the fire beetle?"

"Charles got it," I reassured him, brushing away some of his hair out of his face and gazing into his blue eyes. In the light of the orb that had been pushed beneath us, he looked tired but also heroic.

Heroic? What nonsense am I thinking, I wondered. I'd been the one to be heroic, I saved his butt, and he had the nerve to look heroic and dashing?

"Thank you," Zack said, averting his eyes. "You really saved me with that shield. Even with it up it got really hot inside; I can't imagine I'd have survived that without you."

"Don't be so rash next time," I said before I could help myself. Zack recoiled at this and shot me a look. I hadn't meant it to sound so mean, but he just got me all frustrated sometimes. With his pretty blue eyes and cute freckled face. I didn't want him to get hurt, I didn't want any of us to be in this situation, but it was what it was.

If we could just pull our talents together and face what lay ahead in a smart, planned out way, then we might just make it back. It was clear what we had to do, find the Elemental Stone and return it to the Crystal mountain. *Why* was still unclear, or how Mr. Shadow had done this to us, also unclear, but we had a path forward and just needed to follow it.

"I need to make traps," Zack said, finally finding his words. "If we set enough rock traps and spike traps, these bugs will be no problem."

"What about the bats?" I asked, remembering how many pairs of eyes we'd seen and knowing we weren't prepared for so many at once. "Traps aren't going to do much against flying bats the size of dogs. Did you even see how big some of those were that flew past us? We are going to need a better plan than just traps."

"Why do you have to be so difficult?" Zack said, surprising me.

I reared back as if struck, looking to Jayden and Sofia for support, but neither met my eyes. I wasn't trying to be difficult, I just wanted to lay out all our problems so we could get real solutions to them. It was important to have all the factors laid out if you were ever going to come up with a real solution to so many problems. I opened my mouth to say just that when Zack kept on talking.

"I'm the leader here, I am going to get us through this. The bats aren't an issue, Charles and I took care of them easily enough," Zack said, and I could tell he was trying to sound confident, but a shake in his voice gave me the opening I needed.

"You aren't our leader; we are a small group that needs to work together. Don't you get it, Zack? We need to lay out our problems so we can find solutions. Now stop taking everything so personal and let's figure out how to get through this cave. The exit is gone, by the way, but there has to be another way out," I said, lowering my voice so as not to let Sofia overhear.

The idea that we were stuck underground in the dark wasn't something I needed to remind her of and I knew that Zack lacked the tact to understand it, so hopefully me lowering my voice would tip him off enough.

He increased the volume of his voice when he next spoke, and I cringed.

"If we are a group that needs to work together then why are you whispering? Even small groups need a leader, a voice to give the final say. I am that voice. Being stuck underground and in the dark isn't a problem, we will work it out. But first we need traps to help us from being overwhelmed. You going to let me make traps or did you want to question me some more?" Zack asked.

I saw Sofia's face go a few shades whiter as she listened to Zack. I shot him a dirty look and went over to her, holding her hand again. The ground beneath my feet was soft, and I nearly stumbled over a dead bug as I made my way to Sofia. Holding her hand tight, I spoke into her ear.

"It'll be alright, we will make it out of this."

CHAPTER 7
ZACK – VICTORY SO SWEET

I didn't know what their deal was, I had a solid plan, and it was going to work. I told myself this while gathering up rocks and supplies I needed to craft my traps. It was pretty easy and straightforward, I just envisioned what I wanted and poof the magic took over. If this was going to work, I needed to set as many as possible.

"We should explore further into that larger room and look for other passageways. I want to put down as many traps as possible before more come—actually!" I said, getting excited toward the end with a new idea.

"Actually what?" Jayden asked, kneeling down beside me while I finished up another trap. He squinted his eyes as the materials warped together into the simple traps I had envisioned. A few, the rock fall ones, had little rock hooks on them that would allow me to attach them to the stoney ceiling of the cavern. Not so many rocks to block us in, but enough to bring down a bat for sure.

"What if I set this entire hallway with traps, then we lure the bats and insects into it. You could all stay back, and I will make a path that I can run to get back. Yes, this is going to work!" I said, the excitement of the idea growing on me every second.

"That sounds really dangerous for you," Addy said, her pretty brown eyes fixed on me. I got distracted for a few moments just looking at her, but eventually I recovered enough to hear her words.

Too dangerous for me? What did she know about what I could handle? This wasn't so dangerous; I'd thought about everything that could go wrong. Even if a whole bunch came after me, none of them had been particularly fast. I could out speed any of them if it came down to it and I knew it!

"I'll be fine," I finally said, shaking my head at the lack of faith she had in me.

"It isn't about you being fine," Addy shot back, a bit of heat had entered her voice and it caught me off guard. "You will put us all in danger if you fail. We need to think of a better solution. Maybe we can dig ourselves out of the cave and then collect enough hides to make armor for everyone. There are other options, we just need to find them."

"Whatever," I said, deciding to ignore her. I'll do my

plan and prove to them I have what it takes to be their leader. "Jayden, help me clear the bugs to the side."

Jayden jumped up and together we cleared the hallway of bugs and what little Charles left of the bats. It was dirty work, but I didn't mind it. My shirt had all but had enough of the dirt and grime, my mom would be furious at me if she saw the state of it. My mother... I hadn't thought too much about her but now that I did, I felt a touch of wetness enter my eyes.

In all the adventures I'd seen, no one ever missed their mother, it was always adventure, adventure, adventure. But now that I was in the middle of my own fantasy adventure, I couldn't help but wonder how she was doing. She must have missed me by now... Sure she had! She'd be giving the school and that Mr. Shadow a good piece of her mind. No one messed around with my mother and got off without hearing an ear full.

"Love you mom," I whispered beneath my breath when I was far enough away from the group. "I'm coming back, don't you worry." The words lit a fire in my chest. I would get back and no one, not even Addy, would stand in my way.

With the area cleared, I got to work getting the traps in place. I was just a touch too short to get the ceiling traps set up, and they required a string to be pulled, so I used Jayden to help lift me up a bit and I got them all into place. All the while, the girls talked amongst themselves and I wondered at what they were saying. Probably going over all the things they thought I was doing wrong or something. Girls, who needed them!

The cords wove together in bunches of three and I turned to Jayden to give him instructions.

"So, here's the deal," I said, taking one of the cords in hand. "All you have to do is pull them and bam the trap comes down. But don't pull until I'm clear, got it?"

"Obviously," Jayden said, smiling at me with a little sarcastic turn of his lips. "I've got it and for what it matters, I believe in you. You got this. But promise me one thing."

"What's up?" I asked, letting the string fall to the ground and stepping onto the small path I'd set up for myself. It was all marked by rocks, so the group knew not to go too far ahead or where not to step. As gross as it was, I'd used some of the bug guts to mark my path, dipping the rocks in the green goo.

"Take Charles with you. I've communicated well enough where he can step and I think he understands," Jayden said, and as if to prove his point Charles jumped around me into the path where it was safe to walk. He barely fit with his steps, but he was careful not to nudge any traps.

"That's a good idea," Addy said, coming up from behind us and startling me.

"Of course it is," I said, shooting her a look. "Jayden's a genius. Okay I'm ready, this might get a bit crazy, so everyone check that you have full energy on your bracelets. Jayden, be ready to temporarily tame any bugs that make it through, that'll allow you guys an extra line of defense. Only start attacking after the traps have done their job, got it Addy?" I asked, turning to her specifically as she had the most combat focused abilities. It annoyed me a bit that I didn't get the cool Green Lantern style bracelet, but I had to admit I loved being able to craft things out of stuff. It helped that I always was taking things apart and trying to put them back together. It gave me a sense for what I could create and what I couldn't, even here.

"Got it," Addy said flatly, returning the look I was sending her.

I moved out through the line of traps with Charles right behind me, breathing heavily. It was a bit unnerving being with the dinosaur alone, but Jayden assured me that he would stay tamed no matter the distance as long as he was fed. This should have put me at ease, but the hungry look Charles gave me when I looked over my shoulder sent tingles down my spine.

"Nice, dino," I said, catching its eyes. "You don't want to eat me when I am going to find all sorts of bats for you, right?"

Charles nodded his head at me, as if saying yes. There was a true intelligence in his eyes I realized, and I wondered if he actually had understood me without the aid of Jayden translating his thoughts and impressions. He nudged me in the arm when I stood staring ahead for a solid minute, wondering how fast I'd need to run. It startled me back into action and I started forward at a jog.

No sooner had I made it into the larger room than did the ground start shaking and red eyes from above began to appear. The race was on, but I couldn't flee too fast or too soon, because I needed to NOT lose them while I ran.

Charles made a screeching sound at them, as if daring them to challenge us, and the screech of many bats answered his call. At least a dozen bats came swooping down at us, just as bugs by the dozens began to appear all around.

I slashed out at a centipede that appeared in our path as Charles and I turned to run. It came apart and I nearly slipped on its guts but managed to steady myself. We ran like the wind, Charles slowing enough that he never really left me behind but led the way back to Jayden without hesitation. The small light globe I had gave me enough to see where to step, but not much more. Screeching and clicking followed closely behind me and I knew my feet weren't going fast enough.

Just when I heard the clicking get closer than I wanted it to be, Charles broke off and leapt into the heap of insects, slashing with his feet and biting with his massive maw.

"No!" I screamed, turning but not stopping. "Come on Charles, Jayden needs you!"

But the mass of bugs had already swarmed over the raptor, and it wasn't looking good for him. What did I do?

Should I turn back and fight or keep running? Emotions washed over me and then I felt Ash move on my shoulder, flying forward at the mass of bugs.

A sudden terrible sense of fear and loss washed over me, and I dove forward to save my poor Ash from any harm. Slashing and yelling I fought back ants, beetles, even a few spiders the size of a dog. Ash returned to my shoulder and a sense of warmth washed through me just as Charles jumped free of the horde of bugs, covered in blood and bug guts.

One look from him told me all I needed to know. It was time to run and run fast. With speed unlike I'd ever summoned before, I ran alongside Charles toward our trap hallway. Speed and luck were with us as we turned a corner and, in the distance, saw our friends' faces lit up by globes of light.

CHAPTER 8
ADDY – RIDDLES AND TRAPS

I released barrage after barrage of hard light javelins into the oncoming horde, careful to hit the ones that stepped where traps had already been triggered. Charles, looking worst for wear, and Zack had made it through the line of traps and now fought against the rising horde that he'd lured our way.

The battle was fierce, but Zack had been right, the traps took care of most of the bugs and even a fair bit of the bats. I couldn't tell if the bats were even an issue, Charles jumped up and ate them down as fast as they came.

After a time, the plan succeeded, and the horde of bugs and bats were defeated. The tunnel was a mess of bug guts and rock debris, but not a single one of us felt like cleaning it up just yet. I collapsed next to Sofia, the drain of using up all my bracelet energy taking more out of me than I cared to admit.

"You feeling okay?" I asked Sofia, her face looked a tad bit green in the low light of my orbs. She'd participated more than I thought she was going to, swinging her sword with expertise, and cutting down a bat and three bugs in total. But whatever the effects of the attack had been, she wasn't dealing with it well.

"I'm so scared," she whispered just loud enough for me to hear and no one else. Her hand trembled then and I saw just how bad she was doing. Then just as fast as the trembling started, it stopped, and she got a relaxed look on her face. I noticed her snake slithering around her shoulders and guessed at what had happened.

"We should talk about these mechanical companions," I announced, convinced now that I knew what they were doing to us.

I looked over to Cappy, my precious monkey hanging off my shoulder, and I almost changed my mind, but it had to be put out in the open.

"What are you going on about?" Zack asked, not even looking up from where he fiddled with some items to make another trap.

"What is there to talk about?" Jayden said, reaching down and petting his mechanical fox. "Neil has been a wonderful companion. I'm even beginning to think he is able to soothe my emotions, which helps because I know I should be terrified of so much of what is happening."

"That's just it," I said, looking at Cappy and ignoring the flush of soothing emotions that hit me at that moment. "Our emotions are being played with; shouldn't we be more wary about random robot creatures that happen to look like old pets? Like seriously, what is going on here?"

Zack looked at his bird, he'd named it Ash I think, and tilted his head to the side while regarding it. "Ash wouldn't mess with me like that..." Zack began to say but stopped mid-sentence.

"You've felt it too, haven't you?" I asked, not wasting a moment.

"I... well yeah, I guess I have," Zack said, looking at his mechanical bird as if it were something rather than a friend. "What the heck you dang bird."

Then, as I sat there thinking of what to say next, an emotion and words entered my mind.

The feeling of pure calmness came over me and by the looks of the others, they felt it too.

...We are here to aid you against the Shadow. Do not reject our help, for we can help push back the darkness...

The voice in my head was friendly yet held a sense of weird strangeness that I couldn't understand. Cappy nuzzled into my neck, and I sighed, giving in to the little guy. He seemed tired now, curling up in a ball. Whatever he'd done, whatever all of them had done, it had made them tired. Each of them curled up and seemed to be sleeping.

"I trust them," Sofia said. "My snaky poo would never hurt me."

"I also find myself trusting them," Jayden said, pushing his glasses up on his nose to better see. "Whatever they've just done, and I am assuming you all felt and heard it, they didn't have to do it I don't think. They used much of their power to send us a friendly message and I'm taking their word on it."

"I mean, who else have we met that wants to help us," Zack cut in looking at me with an odd sort of pleading in his eyes that I couldn't remember seeing from him before. It was like he wanted me to accept the little helpers so he could. Surely the confident joker Zack didn't need my okay to trust his little companion?

"Fine," I said, looking to each of my friends in turn. "I trust them too, but we should be careful. Changing someone's emotions isn't safe, I'm sure my father would have lots to say on the subject if he were here. Mother would be going wild if she knew I was trusting an emotionally adjusting mechanical monkey. Yeah, I think I'm going to have to keep this entire adventure to myself when I get back, otherwise I'll never get my chance to become a doctor."

"If we make it back," Sofia said, she hung her head, but her words were like cold ice.

"Let's rest up and head out after we finish clearing up this mess. I think one or two more rounds like this, and we will have cleared the cave," Zack said, trying to take charge once more. "Sofia, you think you can store all the bug parts? I think I might be able to make something from them later."

"Eww gross," Sofia said without hesitation.

I didn't feel like arguing and fell into a rhythm of helping clear bug parts, resting, and thinking. There was so much going on that I didn't know how to handle it and with Cappy sleeping I wasn't getting the overwhelming sense of peace anymore so I could focus on working it out in my head.

Somehow our substitute teacher, Mr. Shadow, had sent us to an island untouched by mankind. Yet every turn we made we found signs of people living here before us, from the cave-like paintings to the Latin words scrawled all over the place. Zack told Mr. Shadow that we wanted to come here, really this was his fault and he had yet to own up to it. Instead, he tried to boss everyone around and be 'the leader'. And what for? So, he could feel a little better about himself? Just thinking about it made me angry and I accidentally crushed the remains of a beetle shell, the kind Zack wanted to save so he could try and make armor or something.

"Easy there," Zack said, scooping up the cracked remains. "If I can pull this armor off, we are going to need every piece we can get."

I closed my eyes and took a deep breath. Then opening them, I walked over to Sofia and sat down next to her. She'd been taking another break, and I was done helping at the moment, so I would take another break as well.

Clean-up finished shortly after, and the traps were laid out once more. We repeated the pulling of bugs and bats four times before the larger room was cleared, but only the first time were we almost overrun. Each one afterward had fewer and fewer bugs and almost no bats. Charles was happy to feast on the bats and we triggered the rock fall traps on bugs instead. It would be some time before that raptor would be hungry again.

When we finally had the large room cleared, we all left and began to explore, looking for additional tunnels and ways out. What we found instead was a door covered in Latin on the furthest wall. It had several riddles written into it, none of them made any sense.

Trying my best I answered them in Latin, speaking aloud to see what would happen.

"Oh no," I said, grimacing as the room began to shake and rocks started to fall from the ceiling.

"Into the door," Zack yelled, as it slid open just enough for one person to squeeze in at a time. To my surprise, Zack slipped through first, some leader he was. Just as I walked forward to go next, the door slammed shut and the shaking got worse.

"Look for another way out!" I yelled and we began running in the dark, following the side of the wall to stay out of the way of the falling debris. A sense of soothing calm tried to wash over me, but I was far too anxious for it to work. I looked at Cappy and gave him a reassuring smile for trying to help.

Just as I was about to give up hope we came across a wide and tall opening in the rock. Without a second's thought the three of us rushed into it.

Breathing hard, but safe from the falling debris, we looked at each other in the dim light.

"We lost Zack," I said, and noted that both Jayden and Sofia looked as horrified as I felt.

CHAPTER 9
ZACK – ALONE AND AFRAID

I gripped the tiny ball of light tight in my hands as I looked around the narrow hallway that I found myself in. What was I thinking rushing headlong into the door by myself? I was just so scared and ready to be the hero, finding the way out for all of us.

"Can you hear me!" I yelled at the backside of the door for the hundredth time, but no answer came. I was alone, in the mostly dark, with a robotic bird that I wasn't really sure I could trust anymore.

Ash nuzzled at my face, and I smiled at him.

"I'm just kidding buddy, of course I can trust you," I said, then looking around the tunnel I decided I had to go forward, there was no other way.

"Do you think they even miss me?" I asked Ash, but he didn't respond, instead a heavy sense of peacefulness washed over me as I took the forward path step by step.

Despite the soothing peace I felt, there was one other emotion that wouldn't leave me alone. Fear. The light I held began to flicker, getting to the end of its life and suddenly Sofia's fear of the dark didn't seem like such a bad idea. The last thing I wanted was to be alone in the dark.

The light went out and I was forced to follow the wall with my hands feeling the way forward. Waves of unwanted fear washed over me, and I felt tears begin to well up in my eyes.

"No," I told myself, not bothering to keep quiet. "You are strong, and you can do this."

My hand ran over something soft on the wall around the same time that my feet stumbled on something on the ground, it sounded like sticks, but it was so hard to see. I picked it up. It was smooth to the touch and had rounded ends. Closing my eyes and hoping for the best, I took the soft stuff off the wall of the cave and tried to combine it with the stick I'd found, hoping I'd be able to make a torch.

It resisted at first, but I put my entire willpower into the task and bam, suddenly I had a flickering torch in my hands, burning with an unnatural blue flame. Checking my bracelet, I learned what I'd crafted. It was a spectral torch, and the ingredients were cave moss and bones.

I nearly dropped the torch when I realized I was holding a bone from a person, or dinosaur or something. Looking on the ground I saw that the entire area was littered with piles of bones, the skulls showing me that they were most likely some form of medium-sized dinosaurs.

"Take a deep breath and stay calm. You have light, now just focus on what more you can do," I told myself as I inspected the walls. There was some color variation in the stone that had blueish streaks mixed into the dark brown. I'd played enough video games to know this was the color of copper, or at least it was in some survival games I'd played.

Grabbing some more bones and stone, I fashioned a pickaxe. My own had been left behind with Sofia, only my sword making it through the door with me. But luck was on my side again and I was able to fashion a pickaxe or rather a spectral pickaxe.

I leveled my new tool and slammed it down on the stone. At first the work was slow, and I got very little of the blue metal. But as I got more out, I saw that it was indeed copper color, a reddish shine to it. The first thing I did was create another pickaxe out of the new metal; it was still a spectral pickaxe, but it had the added benefit of being made from a harder metal. Soon I was pulling out more copper than I knew what to do with in the short length of tunnel.

I started with a sword, this time what I created was a proper sword, no half wood half stone, but full metal. Next, I fashioned some armor and even a few advanced traps that opened up after getting access to the copper.

"See Ash," I said, turning to Ash after covering myself with a lite-style of copper armor. How I'd been able to do it without leather, I did not know, but the armor worked, covering most of my body. "We don't need anyone after all. I will find this elemental stone and be the hero, you just watch."

CHAPTER 10
ADDY – PUSHING FORWARD

"We have to go back for him!" Jayden said, wringing his hands as he spoke. I looked at him and could see he wasn't going to take no for an answer, but there was one small problem.

"We can't," I said, my eyes finding the ground more interesting. I'd look anywhere but in his face at that moment.

"Why not?" Sofia asked, surprising me by speaking up. I hadn't really thought that she'd care to try and find Zack, not that she was cold-hearted or anything. She was always more focused on herself, so it surprised me to see any level of concern coming off of her for someone she obviously doesn't like. But none of that mattered because my light was showing me something the others had failed to see.

"The way back is blocked, look at the rocks down the

tunnel, there is no getting out the way we came," I explained.

They both looked now, and I focused on the globe of light in my hand, increasing the power in it to really give them a good look. The light poured out and illuminated our predicament. Stones the size of Charles were pressed together so tightly that I couldn't see even a peep of what lay beyond.

Jayden stared at the rocks, then turned and looked down the dark tunnel that was our only way forward. Taking a deep breath and closing his eyes, I could see him going over the reality of our situation. Jayden was strong, Zack teased him a bunch, but I could see the strength in him working as he considered what ought to be done next.

"I'm going to go on ahead with Ch-Charles," Jayden said, his voice cracking as he spoke. "Once I've made sure it's safe, I'll come back for you both."

"No," Sofia said, surprising me again. She spoke firmly and held the sword in her hand as if ready for battle. "We go together. We have to stay together."

"I agree," I added.

Jayden didn't seem put off by this, in fact, his entire attitude changed, and he smiled.

"I'm so glad you think that because I was not looking forward to going off on my own. We are stronger as a unit," Jayden said, adjusting his glasses further up his nose as he stood tall at the head of the group, his raptor peered into the distance as if seeing something only he could see.

"Zack should have learned that," Sofia said, shaking her head. "I can't believe he is gone. Will we be able to find him?"

I really didn't know how to handle this sudden change in Sofia, like she was showing she cared about Zack in a way I didn't expect. Putting a hand on her shoulder, I pulled her into a hug just as she melted into a sobbing mess. "It'll be okay," I lied. "Zack is a smart kid; he will figure out a way back to us. And who knows! Maybe the way forward intersects with the path he took."

"Get ready," Jayden said, his voice shaky. "Charles senses something ahead."

We waited with breaths held for a solid five minutes before I turned to Jayden with a questioning look. He just shrugged.

"Let's get moving, weapons out and—here, let me refresh your light globes before they go out," I said, casting several new balls of light just as the former ones winked out.

Zack would be all alone and in the dark now. But he was resourceful, that much was true. If any member of the party had what it took to survive alone for a while, it had to be Zack. Suddenly I felt tears of my own welling up in my eyes, but I pushed them back. What the team needed right now was a strong leader and I could take that role if I needed to.

"Move out," I said, taking point with Charles at the front of the group.

It was because of my positioning and the bright swath of light that went before me, that I saw something cross right in front of us some twenty feet ahead. It was as if the very walls moved and shook the earth. Stumbling from the sudden shake, I almost lost control of the light ball I'd conjured. I had to look away for only a second to refocus on holding it in my hand, but in that small amount of time the moving wall some twenty feet ahead had gone, leaving only darkness.

Charles growled and my breathing turned raspy as my heart began to beat faster.

"Som-something is right ahead, but I can't tell what," I called over my shoulder, taking one slow step after another.

No one answered me, but I could almost hear their heartbeats racing alongside my own as we approached the mysterious area. But all we found was an intersection in the tunnel, just as perfectly round and rough as the tunnel we currently walked in. Had something large been moving through the tunnel and I mistook it for a wall? That would have to be something pretty big to come off as a wall. Then with a sudden rush of dread I realized what these tunnels must be. Not tunnels at all, but burrows. Something big, long, and monstrous lived down here, and we were walking through its tunnels.

"I think we should hurry," I said, using all my force of will to keep my voice from trembling.

We began to jog forward, always forward, despite coming across several intersections. The way forward had the slightest upward angle and I wanted out of this place, so up and up we would go.

CHAPTER 11
ZACK – FINDING A WAY

I was a lone wolf, on the path of victory. At least that's what I told myself as I killed yet another pack of giant ants in the square tunnel I walked down. The further I got the less enemies I seemed to encounter, but it didn't matter to me. With my new copper armor, even when I got scratched it didn't make it past my defenses. I found some discarded cloth and was pulling a good amount of ore behind me, along with bug parts.

Some of the bug parts went into making some cool shoulder armor that I envisioned, with little spikes on it and everything. Life was going good, so why did I feel so crappy?

"Hey Ash," I said, looking over at the almost always quiet bird. I'd taken up a habit of talking to him, despite the fact that he didn't talk back much at all. "We need to find the group, don't we?"

Ash didn't answer, but I took the look he gave me for what it was.

"I know what I said before, but I care about them, they're my friends."

I stumbled on a bit of rock on the ground but caught myself by touching the nearby wall.

"Sure, even Sofia," I said, pretending like Ash had given me a response. "I mean, going solo was fun at first, but I'm worried about them."

That is when the light of my torch hit a doorway ahead. Not any doorway, but one with that silly Latin on it that I couldn't read. Walking up to it I touched the door, pushing on it. No good, the door was stuck fast.

"Well, where do I go now?" I asked no one in particular.

For my trouble I got a soothing rush of emotions from Ash, then the ground started to rumble.

"Great, now what?" I asked the tunnel as rocks began to fall all around me. Suddenly, something huge broke through the wall and I was jumping for cover towards the doorframe. It didn't open for me, but appeared to be sturdier, so for the time being I was safe.

All around me dust had been kicked up so I could no longer see the thing that had broken straight through the rocks, but as the sound of rocks crunching went away, so did a touch of my fear. The tunnel seemed stable after the shaking stopped and whatever had come close to getting me was well on its way to someplace else.

The dust settled and I held my torch up to examine the damage. Pushing down my worries, I saw that, seemingly out of nowhere, a six-foot round tunnel had appeared that went both left and right, out of the main square tunnel. Realizing that I'd never get through the door by myself, I decided to follow the new path, however there was no way I was going to go right. To the right, whatever had made this tunnel awaited me, it would be better to go the already traveled route and hope I didn't meet any of its friends.

Walking up to the opening and biting down on my lip, I took several deep breaths. This was the way, I told myself. Sure, it had been made by some kind of giant burrowing monster, but perhaps it connected to other parts of the cave system, it was worth a shot. I gathered up my bundle, held my torch out before me, and walked onward.

With each step I traveled, I moved further from the safety of a well-crafted tunnel and into the unknown. After a time of walking and looking behind my shoulder in fear of the monster returning, I reached a fork in the tunnel.

"Left, right, or straight?" I asked Ash, hoping that this time at least he might have an answer for me.

"Squawk!" Was his only response. What kind of parrot, robotic or otherwise, made such noises? Silly bird.

"I want to choose the right path, so I will go right!" I said, laughing at my own little bit of word play. There was no one here to really appreciate it, but it left me smiling.

After another right, two lefts, and a straight, I found myself thoroughly lost and at a dead end.

This particular dead end was not the first I'd encountered but it was the most annoying. My last turn had been close to an hour ago, with no other branches and now I was stuck with the prospect of having to turn back and walk that hour all over again.

Then an idea struck me as I looked at the loose rocks blocking my way. The very top appeared to be open to the other side, though not big enough for me to get through. What if I could fashion some kind of trap that would leverage the rocks out of the way? I had a hard time envisioning what that might look like, but I got to work using what I had on hand to see if it were even possible.

"One way or another, I'm moving forward," I told Ash, a look of grim determination settling over my face. "I'm coming back, guys. Don't give up on me yet."

CHAPTER 12
ADDY – ELEMENTAL STONE

The burrowed tunnels led us in random directions, but finally it paid off. After what felt like hours of jogging through and not seeing or feeling any sign of life, we reached a massive twenty-foot-high ceiling square tunnel with a really big stone double doors set into the wall. The other direction was a hallway that only went about ten feet before it was all collapsed rock.

"It's Latin!" I exclaimed to my group members, seeing words around the door similar to the riddle door. "Procede et bravium vindica."

"And what does that mean?" Sofia asked, she was getting more and more sassy as the day went on. We hadn't stopped for food yet, which I figured was part of why she was so upset.

"Let's eat while I think about what it means," I said, sending Sofia my best friendly smile.

Of course, I knew that it basically meant proceed and claim your prize or something close to that, but we needed some rest and nourishment. The thought made me think of Zack and how he'd be getting hungry as well, but he didn't have any of the prepared food we'd taken with us inside of Sofia's inventory.

"You've worked out what the words say yet?" Jayden asked, taking some food from Sofia, cooked dodo meat and sharing a bite with his raptor, Charles.

"I think so, but I just want to be sure," I said, the idea of making a mistake right now when it seemed obvious what we'd find on the other side of the wall made my stomach squirm.

"I hope it's a way out," Sofia said between mouthfuls of berries we'd collected.

"I think it might be the room where we'll find the elemental stone," I said sharing my thoughts with the group. "Though I don't know about it being a way out, this isn't a video game where an exit appears at the end of a particularly hard level."

Jayden chuckled and Sofia just looked confused. I honestly didn't get much time to play video games, but I'd taken a summer class about video game design two summers back, it had been my fathers' idea. I didn't actively try to retain any of that information, but sometimes it bled through.

We ate, rested, and after a suitable period of time approached the door. There was no handle, no easy way of getting inside that I could tell, but I reached out and touched the door anyways. Immediately, the words around the door went a brilliant red and then seemed to fade into the rock. Just when I was starting to have a bad feeling about what might be happening, the doors began to swing inward. It was slow moving but after a time the room beyond lay before us.

It wasn't dark like all the others, but instead globes of light burned bright blue and yellow all around the outer edge of a room barely big enough to warrant such massive doors. At the very center was a simple stone pedestal which was smooth on the surface and bowled on the top. Inside the small, bowled part was a gem that seemed to glow a variety of colors, ever shifting and moving.

"You don't think this is an Indiana Jones situation, do you?" Jayden asked, stepping forward and squinting his eyes to get a better look.

I'd seen the film, my father enjoyed it, so I knew what he meant. In the film the prize at the end of the traps and challenges had a final trap. Would this be the same situation I wondered?

"Should we switch it out with a rock then?" I asked, remembering they did something similar in the film, though it hadn't worked it might be worth trying for us.

"What are you talking about?" Sofia asked, looking perplexed. "Let's just grab the thing and go."

With that, she waltzed into the room like she owned the joint and picked up the gem before I could stop her.

"Sofia!" I chided her, then held my breath as I waited to see if a trap would appear. But instead of a trap, a section of the wall opened up showing stairs leading upward.

"I found the exit!" Sofia exclaimed and we all moved over to check out the staircase carved into the stone. Perhaps this place was more like a video game than I gave it credit.

"We should be careful, this could be the trap," I warned, but Sofia was already moving up the stairs, having put the stone away in her inventory.

No sooner had we made it onto the steps did the door close behind us, cutting off our retreat. I clenched my teeth in frustration but said nothing. We would make it through this one way or another. It took only five minutes of walking up the steps before we encountered a section that had collapsed in on itself.

"We're trapped," Sofia said, panic clear in her voice.

"The rocks aren't that big, maybe we can move them?" Jayden suggested.

I just looked on in horror. It was clear what had happened, one of the massive underground monsters making the tunnels had come through here and the very bottom had broken down into the staircase. Maybe if we dislodged enough, we'd be able to get up and into the tunnel it had created, surely whatever they were came to the surface at times?

The rocks began to shift, and Charles growled low in

his throat. They were moving, something was above trying to make its way down to us.

"Weapons ready," I said, mimicking Zacks call to arms. "Get ready for anything!" I barely got the words out when rocks fell all around at our feet and a figure fell out of the ceiling toward us.

CHAPTER 13
ZACK – JUST IN TIME

The trap had worked, dislodging much of the rock I had found in my way. However, I was too close and fell into a hole at the bottom of the rocks. Brushing myself off, I looked up and was surprised to find Addy, Sofia, Jayden, and Charles all looking down at me in surprise.

"Hey guys," I said, trying to act relaxed and not overly relieved like I felt.

I'd done it! I'd found my way back to the group! An overpowering sense of joy permeated through me, and several things occurred to me all at once.

For starters, I didn't care about being the leader anymore. I was just glad to have my friends back. Jayden helped me up and I hugged him tightly, then went to each of my group, hugging them in turn.

"I'm sorry," I said, and I meant it. I'd let my desire to

be a team leader and be important overrule what was even more important, my friendship with these three.

The second thing that occurred to me was how hungry I was. My stomach chose that moment to gurgle hard and loud.

"Here, let me get you some food," Sofia said, a glint of tears in her eyes, but I couldn't really tell why.

"Thank you, I'm so hungry I could eat a raptor," I said, looking at Charles with a mock hungry look. He didn't get my joke though and immediately took a step back and growled.

"Easy, easy," Jayden said, calming his companion. "He was just joking. Dude, I can't believe you're back, but also don't you ever rush ahead again! We need to work as a group, no more macho going on ahead stuff."

"I know," I said, the time alone had been enough to assure me of that. "Let me get some of this food down and then I'll move the rest of these rocks with my new trap."

I ate my fill of berries and dodo meat before standing. Addy hadn't said anything to me yet, so I looked at her and smiled. She smiled back and let out a sigh of relief.

"I'm happy you're okay too," she said, then looking at my armor added, "Where'd you get the cool armor?"

"Oh right," I said, then went back to the hole I'd made, pulling down the copper ore I'd collected. "I have enough to make chest plates for each of you and if we find more, I'll make you entire suits." Then, eying Charles, I had an idea. "I might even be able to make Charles some armor if he wants it."

"That would be exceptionally awesome!" Jayden said, adjusting his glasses in excitement.

I scooped up enough copper and began crafting the chest plates, focusing on each person as I made them. They came out perfect fits, strapping in the back despite the lack of leather. All the while the group chatted around me, there was a real air of comfort now that we were all back together. I even managed to split my focus a bit while crafting to join in the conversation.

"So, you all found the stone?" I asked, amazed that it wasn't the first thing they mentioned when I found them.

"Oh yeah, it's right here," Sofia said, holding it up proudly.

I looked at it and my mouth fell open a bit. Reaching out for it, Sofia handed it over. A sudden warmth covered my body, and I knew this stone was powerful, just not why or what it could do. I happened to be holding Addy's chest plate when I grabbed the stone, I felt a whoosh of power move from the stone and into the chestplate that I'd newly crafted. Looking at it closer, I saw the armor now had an iridescent glow to it. The illumination was slight, but noticeable.

"Whoa," Jayden said, fixing his glasses as they slid down his nose from his sudden lurch forward. "How'd you manage that?"

"I don't know," I said honestly. "I just sort of felt some power leave the stone and enchant the armor."

"Let me see that," Addy said, reaching for the armor. I gladly handed it over, it was hers after all, and watched as she squinted her eyes at it.

"Let me have the stone back," Sofia said, reaching out for the elemental stone.

I moved it out of her reach, wanting to try a few more things with it before I gave it up. "Wait, I want to try out something," I said. Sofia frowned at me but said nothing further in protest.

I touched my shoulder plates, made from bug shells, and closed my eyes. The same rush of power happened again, and I felt it connect with not just my shoulders, but all the armor I wore. There was a warmness coming from my armor now and I knew without a doubt I'd just added some kind of enchantment on it. But what it did or how it affected it I couldn't say.

Passing back the gem, I touched my bracelet and a window appeared.

-You've enchanted armor with 'Elemental Boon', giving it resistance to all elements and a 10% bonus to durability. Rare and powerful artifacts can share their power to enchant certain items by transferring a portion of their power.-

. . .

I finished reading the little window and released my bracelet, ignoring the progress I'd made on it, though it was significant. I'd gained at least 2 or 3 levels and unlocked Custom Crafting. I knew all of this just by quick glance, but I was too excited about the enchanting to focus on it.

"My bracelet thing just told me what happened," I said.

Addy took the gem from my hand after setting aside her armor. I looked down at the armor she'd so casually tossed away and then turned back to Addy just as she opened her hand. Just above her hand she formed a ball of orange fire, then with a twist of her wrist it became a crackling ball of lightning, then water, and then dark shifting dirt.

"Whoa, it enhances our abilities," Addy said, then looking up at me she added, "Sorry, what'd your bracelet tell you?"

I huffed out a mouthful of air in frustration and awe, but after a moment I spoke. "Basically, I enchanted the armor by using a portion of the stone's power. It must grant each of us specific enhanced abilities based on our core abilities. You can project light, but with the stone it lets you—"

She cut me off and finished my thought. "It lets me project the elements, really any I can imagine. Watch, I can do ice as well."

Her hand twisted and a ball of ice appeared in her hand, shiny and see through.

We both looked at Jayden when he cleared his throat. "May I see it?" He asked, more politely than I'd ever have asked.

"Sure thing Jayden," Addy said, handing it over.

Jayden held it for a second, then when nothing happened, he seemed to deflate. Meanwhile Charles looked on, tilting his head to the side while staring at the stone in Jayden's hand.

An idea occurred to me, and I nudged Jayden. "Try touching Charles and see if it effects your current tamed creatures?" I asked, he nodded and held out his hand.

Charles pushed himself into it like a cat that wanted to be pet and suddenly everything changed.

Charles went from being greenish blue, to a fiery orange and yellow. Even his eyes seemed to burn with fire. Just as I had that thought, Charles opened his mouth to the ceiling and let out a burp of flames. He didn't seem harmed by the process, but Jayden looked confused.

"What's up?" I asked him, he still held a hand on Charles.

"My first thought was fire, you know, to make him look like a dragon or something, but now I can't try any other elements. I feel blocked by the stone," Jayden said, looking perplexed.

"Maybe it's like the enchanting, a one-time thing. Try letting go of Charles and see if the changes stick," I said.

Jayden did so and as I thought, nothing changed. He had permanently changed Charles' element to fire, likely giving him cool fire-based abilities.

"What does it do for you?" I asked Sofia, but she didn't answer, just walking over to Jayden she took it and put it away.

Finally, after we all stared at her for a few seconds she responded. "It lets me see the elemental affinities and other basic information about items in my storage. Nothing special."

I had to agree with her, I didn't think that was so awesome, but Addy shot her a look that seemed to say, 'she should not be so hard on herself'.

We finished resting and finally I pulled out my trap to show off. It was a tool more than a trap, but it worked automatically, using some shells, rock, and other random materials I'd found, including copper to make a spring to wedge into rocks and force them to move. Sort of like scissors but I had a spring in place to help open them and move rocks. It was also about the size of my torso, so I put it in place and demonstrated by moving several rocks larger than my chest.

"If we keep this up, I think we can clear the staircase," I said, moving some more rocks aside. Together we worked, slow and steady, moving away debris and clearing the way of rocks.

CHAPTER 14
ADDY – FRESH AIR

We moved swiftly up the stairs, but my mind lay elsewhere. The power of the elemental stone still lingered on my mind. It pushed away, momentarily, the thoughts and worries about Zack. Now that he was back, we were whole again and I was excited to get this adventure over with.

I summoned an extra ball of light and passed it over to Zack. He took it, smiling at me in the process. My cheeks warmed and I wondered if he noticed in the dim light of the ever-ascending staircase.

Why did I care if he saw me and why was I getting hot in the face anyways? I pushed the questions aside and focused on the elemental stone and what lay ahead of us. We needed to find a way to this Crystal Mountain, and we'd finally be free of this place, able to return back to our lives.

It was an interesting thought, returning back to the old world. This little adventure had been more excitement than I'd ever experienced and now that I had Zack back, I was kind of enjoying myself.

We traveled slow but steady, ever upward until finally we came across a flat room. Inside the flat room was another door, it was ajar and after a bit of looking around and finding nothing, we went through it into a final staircase.

Light, blessed real sunlight, poured in from above and before long we'd made it out and into an open rocky outcropping. It overlooked the beach and far down, maybe a mile or so, I could barely make out our treehouse. We'd done it, we'd escaped the underground caves!

"Finally," I said, turning to the group, each of them showing different levels of excitement.

"Now we just need to get the stone to the mountain and we're good!" Zack said, pumping his fist into the air. "Hey guys, there is something I wanted to say."

"Okay," I said, the others simply nodding toward Zack.

"I'm sorry I tried to take charge and was so focused on being the leader that I wasn't a good team player. I've learned my lesson and I'm here to help in any way as a member of the team, not as the leader," Zack said. I could tell the words weren't easy for him, but I was so proud to hear him say them.

"It's alright to take charge," I said, smiling over to

him. "You just have to be open to hear from us instead of just shooting out orders. What if we vote on who should call the shots? I'll start, I vote for Zack."

"But I really don't want to lead anymore," Zack said, surprising me.

"That might help you be a better leader," Jayden said. "I vote Zack as well."

"Me too," Sofia said, her face flushing red as she looked over to Zack.

CHAPTER 15
ZACK – NEW ADVENTURE AWAITS

I didn't know what to think about the turn of events. They really wanted me to be their leader and call the shots after all I did? It took me some time, but I nodded my head and accepted the decision of the group.

"I accept," I said. "But if you change your minds, let me know. I'm just happy to be able to help out."

Turning and looking over the horizon, I saw the Crystal Mountain far in the distance. We had a long way to go but we'd make it if we worked together and didn't let silly things get in our way.

"So, shall we go back to our base camp and start getting supplies for our Journey to Crystal Mountain?" I asked.

"Lead the way," Addy said, smiling at me and making my face warm.

Blushing and thinking how pretty Addy was in the

full light of the sun, I started my way down toward the beach. We made it without incident to the home base and began to prepare for the final leg of our adventure.

It hadn't been a long journey just yet, but I'd learned so much. We need to work together and support each other, like friends should.

The End of Book 2 of Journey to Crystal Mountain

LEAVE A REVIEW

Thank you for reading. Please leave a review.

Check out my website at AuthorTimothyMcGowen.com

If you really liked the book, please consider reaching out and telling me what you enjoyed about it at, Timothy. mcgowen1@gmail.com.

Join my Facebook group and discuss the books at: https://www.facebook.com/groups/234653175151521/

Join my Patreon at: https://www.patreon.com/TimothyMcGowen

ABOUT THE AUTHOR

Timothy McGowen was born in Modesto, California. His journey into stories started with reading the Goosebumps books. Later he read a novel by Terry Brooks and became hooked on fantasy/scifi almost instantly. Shortly after that he was given a school assignment to write a 5 page fiction story, and 25 pages later his story was half done. He hasn't stopped writing since.

His popular Arcane Knight series has sold thousands of copies in both ebook and audible so far. Consider signing up for my newsletter for news on book releases as they become available.

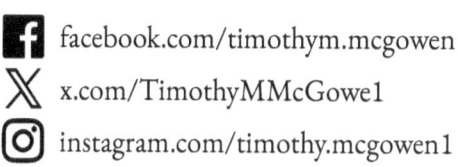

facebook.com/timothym.mcgowen

x.com/TimothyMMcGowe1

instagram.com/timothy.mcgowen1

LITRPG GROUP

Check out this group if you want to gather together and hear about new great LitRPG books.

(https://www.facebook.com/groups/LitRPGGroup/)

LEARN MORE ABOUT LITRPG/GAMELIT GENRE

To learn more about LitRPG & GameLit, talk to author and just have an awesome time by joining some LitRPG/Gamelit groups.

Here is another LitRPG group you can join if you are looking for the next great read!

Facebook.com/groups/LitRPG.books

List of LitRPG/Gamelit Facebook Groups:

- https://www.facebook.com/groups/LitRPGReleases/
- https://www.facebook.com/groups/litrpgforum/
- https://www.facebook.com/groups/litrpglegends/
- https://www.facebook.com/groups/LitRPGsociety/
- https://www.facebook.com/groups/AleronKong/

www.ingramcontent.com/pod-product-compliance
Lightning Source LLC
Chambersburg PA
CBHW052008170626
46808CB00007B/2839